A BETTER WORLD

HOPE FROM AFRICA

A BETTER WORLD

HOPE FROM AFRICA

A collection of poems by
young leaders across Africa

A Better World: Hope from Africa

First published by Theart Press in 2019
www.theartpressbooks.com
Copyright © Theart Press

ISBN: 978-0-6399373-5-9

Edited by Taryn Lock
Set in Adobe Jensen Pro and Fontin Sans
Page design and typesetting by Theart Press

Dedicated to US President Barack Obama

THEART
Press

Written by members of the
2018 Obama Foundation African Leaders Program

This book contains poems by 37 young leaders
from 15 African countries who all share a
common hope for a better world.

*A special word of thanks to the following
for helping to make this book possible:*

2018 Obama Foundation African Leaders
Obama Foundation
Patrick Freeman
Athol Williams
Taryn Lock
Theart Press

Foreword

The poet, W.B. Yeats, described his landmark book, A Vision, as "a last act of defense against the chaos of the world." He knew the power that poetry possessed to set the world on a hopeful path. While Yeats' book might have been his last defense, in this poetry collection these young African leaders not only present a new defense against the wrong in the world but more importantly, give wings to seeds of great hope.

Just as their work calls and nudges us closer to the world we dream of, so do these leaders' poems. They see the world "pregnant with possibility" and express an impatience like seeds impatient to be released to the soil. They look to humanity with "unshakeable resolve to help her soar." These leaders know that inspiring just one child can make a world of difference, that we walk into the infinity of "blue skies" with simple acts of love. And as all great leaders have done through the ages, these poems express the courage to stand naked in truth, to say: "this body is my story" and though it tells a story of struggle it also tells a story of hope.

It is encouraging that these young leaders have turned to poetry to share their visions of a better world, for poetry offers us a language where our other languages fail. Poetry always has the power to call us closer to the light no matter how deep the darkness, to nudge us closer to the shore no matter how chaotic the seas.

These poems and these leaders speak with the African drumbeat felt underfoot and emulate our centuries-old oral traditions; they remind us that it is never too late to reach out, to take a step and to take a stand.

And so these young men and women join John F. Kennedy in realising the magical ways in which poetry works to change the course of humankind; it is Kennedy who said, "when power narrows the areas of man's concern, poetry reminds him of the richness and diversity of his existence." It is this richness of existence that these poems hold as their guide, and so make this a worthy read for anyone who shares the hope of a better world and a greater humanity.

Athol Williams, poet and social philosopher
Cape Town, South Africa

CONTENTS

dreaming without limits

By Simidele Adeagbo
(Nigeria)

DREAMING WITHOUT LIMITS
by Simidele Adeagbo

It started by daring to dream.
On an ice track, doing what had never been seen.

Being the first and blazing a trail.
Determined and focused, with no option to fail.

Breaking barriers every step of the way.
And showing everyone just how African queens sleigh.

Shifting the narrative on the world's biggest stage.
Refusing to keep our dreams in a cage.

Our dreams are valid, no matter where we're from.
And we all have the power to overcome.

So why not you? And why not now?
Create the future and make us say Wow!

milédou - together as one

By Jean-Luc Agboyibo
(Togo)

MiLéDou - TOGETHER AS ONE
by Jean-Luc Agboyibo

The first call hit like a heart attack,
The last blasted like a knockout,
8 years to get out of the dark,
8 years sharing tender breakfast.

Yam and Coke better than Wifi,
Yawo and Kossi connected by love,
Facing death taught us to forgive,
Missing mothers pushed us to believe.

Source of empathy and compassion,
An ever growing strength,
Welcomed by the inner self,
An awareness that can't be pretended,
An emotional process that requires a guiding star,
To find out who we are.

I launched MiLéDou to nourish our roots.
"we're together", it means.
I want to give back, create a community,
Growing roots, giving wings.
MiLéDou also means "you're together",
A whole self, as our ancestors, who were wise and woke.

Becoming our whole self, is the priority,
Because it is the road to humanity,
Me accepting my vulnerability,
They say I am mentally white like Barry,
But Barry's fight for hope is the key to our personal maturity.

A journey started with simple drills,
Driven by passion and crazy dreams,
Now they consider us as game changers,
Our real victory is inspiring change makers.

We stayed too long in the shadow,
We were hushed by dead souls,
Silenced by our traumas,
Now it's the time to redesign,
In our ways, to shine.

MiLéDou

Photo supplied by MiLéDou

i
am

By *Edith Amin*
(Malawi)

I AM
by Edith Amin

I am not broken just bent
From all the "buts" you whisper at high tables
And unqualified limits you set before me.
Look! These whites can be whiter and your lights brighter.

I promise I can stand straight
My steady back can hold
The much answerability and this parade can be merrier

I am the missing piece
These loops need me
These hoops won't fit I am the jigsaw to slide into place.
Let me fix you, you do not make sense without me.

the
spark

By Amanda Blankfield-Koseff
(South Africa)

THE SPARK
by Amanda Blankfield-Koseff

A spark ignites in a young mind
The possibility, hope and power has been partially
revealed
It is a simple mindshift, from being
Stuck
Bound
Resigned
Helpless
Downtrodden
Which points to a future of inequality. Poverty. Pain.
Sameness.

Then the shift comes:
The mind transforms into a blank canvass where
Creativity
Inspiration
Empowerment
Motivation
Values
Catalyse a new future that starts
Now!
With you...
With me...
Together solving problems innovatively
As active citizens of our beautiful countries.

break
it
down

By Dr Shakira Choonara
(South Africa)

BREAK IT DOWN
by Dr Shakira Choonara

A mess
Too many excuses
Too many wrongs
The expense is ours
Self-created power
Power not from the people
Truth be
Youth become old
Youth begin to be those despised
Distaste
The cycle begins
The end of it must come
Early on
Forever
For our people
Serve but seek not to take.

change

By *Moses Chubili*
(Zambia)

CHANGE
by Moses Chubili

To love, and not to hate
To embrace and not to exclude
To give smiles and not scars
Uniting and not dividing
To stand and not to fall
Leaders making the world an envision of visions
we all want the world to be
Bringing, changing
Changing countries, changing lives, bringing hope
Of a world we want to be
and life goes on and forth.

a
better
world

By Yaya Dama
(Burkina Faso)

A BETTER WORLD
by Yaya Dama

We need a better world

A better world where every child has access to quality education

A better world where every child is happy

A better world where every child can express himself freely

We need a better world

A better world where there is no inequality between people

A better world where people sit together to work

A better world where there is fair partnership between nations

We need a better world

A better world where the sun of peace is shining on the Globe

A better world where there is no war

A better world where there is no ethnic or religious group violence

We need a better world

A better world where there is no artificial borders between countries

A better world where we can travel to any country without visas

A better world where we are one and united

We need a better world

A better world free of corruption

A better world where there is real democracy

A better world where presidential mandates are limited and respected

We need a better world

A better world where quality healthcare is accessible to all

A better world where we have qualified medical personnel

A better world where we have less deaths

We need a better world

A better world where young people trust themselves

A better world where young people have a clear vision of their future

A better world where young people have clear life plans

Yes, a better world

But a better world where we all are ready to change

A better world where we all take actions

A better world where young people are connected and work for positive change

Yes, let's build it together

Yes it is possible

Yes, let's take risks but positive risks

Yes, let's hope together

Where there is hope there is a way

Nothing will work unless we do it

Yes we can, let's build it together.

Photo supplied by the Obama Foundation

the
intrepid

By Paul Ekuru
(Kenya)

THE INTREPID
by Paul Ekuru

Whoa! Whoa! Whoa!
My rifle my companion.
My country my love.
My nation my reason.
My constitution my direction.
This aggression to quench, I will, I will.

Mean-faced I see you.
Suicide-vest you drape.
The presidential palace your aim.
A man innocent, charismatic you kill.
My son your heinous bullet exterminates.
My compatriot in grenade powder he smoulders.

Your reason fickle it is.
Your notion irrational I say.
Your character cowardly it is.
Your soul wretched I bet.
Your life a crime I vouch.
Your ways heartless I deem.
But still we are brothers.
So drop off your grenade, and my rifle I will.
So we may invite peace once and for all.

sacrifice in the name of hope

By Andrew Ihsaan Gasnolar
(South Africa)

SACRIFICE IN THE NAME OF HOPE
by Andrew Ihsaan Gasnolar

All our lives, we are encouraged to believe.
Encouraged to dream, and to do it big.
Yet, there is that part of us that questions.
It often lingers, it bristles but mostly it hurts - that doubt.

Doubt of a real future - questions that always swirl.
Hope birthed in us, birthed by our guardians - watchful, attentive
and always giving. Generous to a fault.

We are able to hold onto their hope - but more so their belief in
who we are because all they showed us is love.
Love before we even had our own life force - even before our
imagination soared.

Lifted up. Pushed beyond our circumstance. Encouraged to forget
- to forget the restlessness of struggle.
Pushed to believe in our opportunity - always loved, and cared for.

The price of this love is sacrifice. Sacrifice hangs over every hug,
push, every opportunity and every chance embraced.
The trick is never to discount that love.

Instead, we must push - push ourselves to remember the price of that love.
Remember it so we can hold ourselves - hold ourselves so that we too can lift others.

Our story resonates - it is full, it is vibrant, it is hopeful. It is the story of Africa - our Africa, where our families rooted for us and sacrificed everything.
A sacrifice that believed in that hope and promise.

We are the future. We are that hope.
A hope that is riddled with sweat, blood and love.
So much love.
Life given to us by our Mothers, Fathers, Grandmothers, Grandfathers, and by our village.

A village that must always remind us about that sacrifice so that we will never falter.
Each step, each moment, each stroke - we carry that love with us.

A love that is far larger than our home, our village and our Africa.
We are that hope - pushed by our truly African soil and blood.
That there is the real promise - that is what we have always waited
for.

A poem for Washielah, my Grandmother, my Hope,

and someone who even in her passing continues to guide and reaffirm.

empathy

By *Temitope Isedowo*
(Nigeria)

EMPATHY
by Temitope Isedowo

I was a treasure hunter
In search of the magic wand
To wave across the sky of the human mind
And clear the existential damage
Of anti-earth politics

In my journeys of discovery
To cultures of the skin and the mind
Across foreign lands and local seas
In sickness and in health
I found no perfect answers or magic wand

All I found was empathy
Laid on the bare cold floor
Shorn of skin and bereft of attention
Relegated to the sidewalk
Of humanity's struggle for sanity

In nurturing empathy, I learned
To become what others are
Without losing my own identity
To put myself in the place of others
To break human glass ceilings

How hard can it be
To show love to the air you breathe
Or the rare, beautiful birds that you see?
How much does it hurt
To love without fixation on colors?

To be liberal or conservative is human
To live without empathy is not.

Photo supplied by the Obama Foundation

equalize

By Joan Kabugu
(Kenya)

EQUALIZE
by Joan Kabugu

I woke up today, feeling dazed,
My new shoes are both for the left leg,
They gave me rejects,
They wouldn't dare give the important man in a three-
piece suit the same,
Yet they shortchanged me.
Oh well, we're not equals.

I woke up today, on the wrong side of town,
My reject shoes walked through unpaved roads,
His perfect shoes didn't get any dust,
Nor does his government Passat, it has access to more
water than I do in a week,
Myself and that car will never be equals.

I woke up today, feeling deflated,
Like a fake helium balloon that won't fill up,
My boss sacked me because my reject shoes are dark
brown and not black,
His boss promoted him after he bribed past a court case,
Really?
My boss and his boss are equals.

I woke up today, and got a call,
My footballer friend from college heard of an opening at his firm,
On the phone, he prepped me for the impromptu interview,
look sharp - he said,
I wore my happy socks and the brownish shoes, I aced it,
I got the job as a cleaner, he bought me a congratulatory lunch,
He introduced me as his friend to his lawyer friends because we are
Equals.

I woke up today, better than most days,
I put on my best tie, an old gift from wifey,
I like my new job, I have a friend, an equal,
My little girl has a shot at a good future,
I'll be the best cleaner there is, heck I'll open a cleaning company
My little girl doesn't need much, just education, food, health and a home,
The Great Equalizers.

Photo supplied by Candace Nkoth Bisseck

let
me
out

By Thulile Khanyile
(South Africa)

LET ME OUT
by Thulile Khanyile

Born out of crisis,
Born out of problems,
Born out of creativity.
A need to close a gap…

I sit in hiding waiting to be blurted out.
I watch, sometimes in frustration as many keep me to themselves.
I listen, as closely as I can to conversations in anticipation of being released.

At times, in conducive rooms and platforms,
With ease I am uttered, discussed and freed from hiding.
Freed from shackles of bondage.
In boardrooms I am the meal consumed on gigantic, shiny tables
Where I offer nourishment and contribution to growth and development.
Nations talk of my power to grow economies.

Why then I ask, would anyone not LET ME OUT?
At times I die a slow death of being ignored until forgotten.
I am an Innovative idea – LET ME OUT!
It may just change the world.

Pregnant with possibility,
Alive with hope.
I am an Innovative Idea!

a
better
world

By Kenyi Yasin Abdallah Kenyi
(South Sudan)

A BETTER WORLD
by Kenyi Yasin Abdallah Kenyi

I want to live in a world
where everyone has the right
to await Freedom,
like all the beautiful mornings
that don't have two cold eyes
scathingly looking at Freedom;

I want to live in a world
where rights to education for women and girls
are promoted and respected in the pastoral community,
while at the same time not waltzing our way
to the grave.
I want to live in a world where forced teenage marriage
after a first menstrual period is abolished and male children
go to school rather than
being forced to keep cattle or get involved in cattle raiding
in other community causing insecurity.

I want to live in a world
in which I can
see a dear,
confident and faithful face
on each step of the way,
instead of those of thousands of conspirators,
tanned tycoons
and stern politicians,
which appear in the street
for two or three weeks a year,

with their lies
like demonic torches
in their cause against people.
I want to live in a world where all people live
in peaceful co-existence where there is
racial and religious tolerance like how Allah
created the universe.

I want to live in a world
where dreaming is dignity
and not a shame,
where there is no need to reconsider
one's importance in the human society,
but it's rather a birthright.

I want to live in a world
where people aren't haunted by conscience
for having once eaten peas,
where food isn't vanity to some
and mere fantasy to others.
I want to live in a world
where we don't bring dandyism
into faith,
to discuss in dandy terms
how mankind no longer has faith;

I want to live in a world
where mankind and faith
walk side by side,
so that even prayers
aren't necessary.

Photo supplied by Obama Foundation

the
african
spirit

By Jonathan Kingwell
(South Africa)

THE AFRICAN SPIRIT
by Jonathan Kingwell

I met two-hundred leaders from the continent
Each so friendly, and quick to compliment
Around the room were two-hundred smiles
Each person unique, two-hundred styles

The projector rolled as leaders' stories were shared
The smiles diminished as their secrets were bared
Each so different, yet we could all relate
So many issues to contemplate

After much debate
We suddenly clicked
We shared one trait
We could not evict

It is the African Spirit in all of you,
It knits our countries together and guides us through

By the end, our minds held one common seed,
To show every single African they were born to lead.

food

By Lucky Komba
(Tanzania)

FOOD
by Lucky Komba

It's such a broad topic, I can't stop thinking about it,
I can only think of one subject, very weird, but very right,
Ever heard of FOOD? Yes, or No, I don't know!

But, let it sink in and think of hunger, then think of a hot plate,
Think of war and bickering, then think of breakfast,
I know what you'll settle for, no fights here, I know.

It's confusing but makes a lot of sense, just imagine,
No getting mad, no bitter minds, no fighting,
Is FOOD the answer? I know you know!

People speak of friendship and love, some speak of happiness and joy,
Prosperity and growth, all-inclusive, some speak of peace and harmony,
Do people speak of FOOD? This one, Yes - I KNOW!

I speak of breakfast, my friend Day speaks of lunch,
Hunger might come so fast, "Sorry friend, I can just settle for a brunch",
I can just leave you with one ask, what's a better world without FOOD?

Food lives in life and death, I know life, I don't know the rest,
Food is satisfaction and brings health, food is freedom and tastes best,
Is FOOD Life? This one, Yes - I KNOW!

I married Happiness because I wasn't a fool, I ate,
I wasn't starving at the altar,
I got my daughter Love because both I and Happiness were full, we ate,
maybe some burger!? Or DINNER, It's funny, I KNOW!

A world with plenty of food is a better world,
   because it's empowering,
A world with plenty of food is a better world,
   because it's fulfilling,
A world with plenty of food is a better world,
   because it's purposeful.

Let's restore humanity and solve our problems,
Let's make more FOOD and make more laughs,
Let's eat, a lot, until we say our goodbyes!

A world with plenty of food is a better one!

Photo supplied by Obama Foundation

here
i
stand
(anderson
street)

By Loyiso Kula
(South Africa)

HERE I STAND
(ANDERSON STREET)
by Loyiso Kula

Clear thought clear mind
I long for my sanity
Clean heart clean Soul
I long for my spirituality
Freed from my darkness
Freed from my anger
I long for a day when I am free from my hunger
The hunger from a freedom I have never known
The hunger from a pain that I know too well
I stand on the street so I can buy my freedom
I am here on these streets so I can no longer hunger
But I know no other way
And I know no other life
I was promised my freedom
I was promised my peace
I stand here and wait for the pain to release.

This poem is inspired by the women who work the streets of Anderson Street,
Johannesburg daily as prostitutes. Their freedom is no longer theirs.

will
you
help
them

By Kudzai Kutukwa
(South Africa)

WILL YOU HELP THEM
by Kudzai Kutukwa

Her mouth is dry as sweat trickles down her brow
Squinted eyes looking towards the horizon but with a frown
Aches coursing through her body as she stands hopeless
The earth is dry, with the heat making her breathless
Motionless in the moment she is, thinking about her reality that is
Will the land yield its increase as is?
Waiting for the rain with hoe in one hand
Wishing away the pain of tilling dry land
Images of her children starving flash across her mind
If the rains don't come, food to feed them will i find?
In the midst of it all one question plagues her mind
Who will help me?

His heart is racing wildly as he finds a place to hide
The footsteps of his pursuers are not far behind
At last he thinks he found a place to seek refuge
But alas they find him before anyone could come to his rescue
On his knees he falls, begging for mercy
"Please I just need a little more time to pay," he cries
His cries fell on deaf ears as fists rained on his face
In his mind's eye he could see himself disappear without a trace
Flashbacks of when he borrowed the money came flooding
All will be well once the rains come pounding he reasoned at the time
Numerous calculations had told him everything would be fine
He remembered the lush green crops he had once imagined
When the rains didn't come, everything turned tragic
His dream became a nightmare and he was now in a tangle

Desperately gasping for air as he was being strangled
in that moment all he had was one question
Who will help me?

Will you help them? Will you raise your hand and say I will help you?
Will you be a voice for the voiceless? Or will you remain silent and
act lifeless?
What can i do to help them? you ask
Am I even up to the task?
Yes you are and yes you can
A better world is possible if you reach out to the vulnerable
If you lend a hand and take a stand, there will be no injustice that can
withstand
A better world begins with the words, "I will help you".

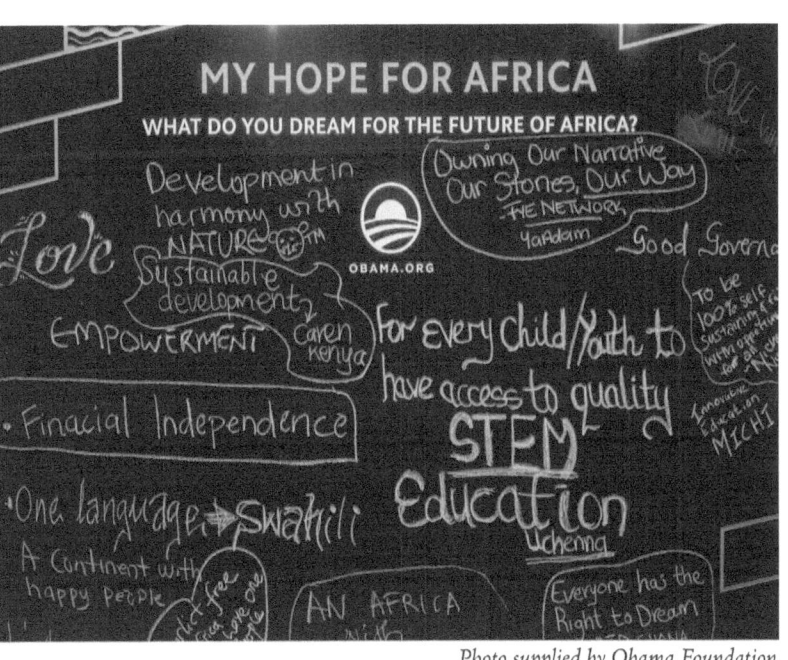

Photo supplied by Obama Foundation

blue
skies

By Taryn Lock
(South Africa)

BLUE SKIES
by Taryn Lock

Seven years old
He wanders home
No dream, no role-model
No book to own

Cape Flats sand
Beneath his soles
Dodging cross-fire
Joining a gang, his goals

His mother a packer
His father unemployed
Destined to do time
Another life destroyed

One day in class
Friendly visitors arrive
With big smiles, fun stories
Encouragement to strive

'Be the best that you can be
And follow your dreams.
Nothing is impossible
No matter how hard it seems.'

They hand him a book
Say it's *his* to keep
Brand new, his first
Oh the benefits society will reap

Excited about his new book
He writes his name inside
Can't wait to show his family
Beaming with purpose and pride

It all starts with reading
We must read... to rise
Education will set us free
With books only blue skies

I dream of a better world
Where every child can read
A nation of inspired readers
Who persevere and succeed

Let's build a thriving nation
A humanity that withstands
I believe we are the ones
The future is in our hands.

me
against
them

By Innocent Magambi
(Burundi)

ME AGAINST THEM
by Innocent Magambi

I remember when I and Chifundo became friends;
it was after a history class on the Bantu people,
great-great-grandfathers we had in common,
discovered with the excitement of a long-lost cousin across the oceans.

The first funeral I attended in Chifundo's village was cool:
I saw multiple sets of triplets – young, old, male, female.
They all looked so alike.
"they are not triplets, they are family,
don't you know that close family members usually look alike?"
explained Chifundo, slightly puzzled at my naiveté.
I nodded, confused and envious at the same time.

When funerals take place in my community,
scores of stand-in cousins, aunties and uncles gather –
but none of them are related to each other.
They are neighbours, church members and people
who help when the wind blows the grass roof off our mud hut.
They are like family, tied together by the commonality of our suffering.
My real family are in different refugee camps, others died in wars.
Though I don't have what Chifundo has, I am not alone, I, too, belong.

In his village and in my section of the refugee camp, drums beat.
Drums beat happy at their harvest time,
drums beat happy after the monthly distribution of our survival rations.

Drums beat relief when a baby comes safely into the world,
at the one clinic that we share, like the school,
between the village and the refugee camp.

Drums beat when Chifundo and I were born,
25 years ago, in that skeletal clinic.
Like brothers from different mothers, we grew up together,
but Chifundo has moved on now.
He is free, got a job in another district –
returns at harvest time to help his family gather
the corn from their ancestral lands.
Me, I dream.
I dream beyond the invisible walls of my confinement.
I dream above the legal restrictions on my freedom of movement, of work,
of voting, of being anything other than a refugee.

I dream one day of Chifundo's people claiming us as their brothers –
descendants of the same forefathers –
I dream of my mother's land proudly calling me home as a legitimate son –
I dream of my unknown father repenting of his violence and rape, and
coming back to find mum and me.

I dream of all of us together,
planting and harvesting,
beating the drum.

I dream of myself rising,
a child of Africa now grown into a man,
keeping out the bad guys who divide us
to create a market for their guns
in exchange with our petrol and gold.

I dream of good neighbours,
helping one another to live
contently within their means.
Our children will no longer be food for ocean creatures,
no longer be the arms and brains that make other nations great.
In my dream, me against them will turn into a strong WE.
WE will lead and the rest will follow.

a
better
world

By Mabatho Makatla
(Lesotho)

A BETTER WORLD
by Mabatho Makatla

A better world
Doesn't exist without love
Love, a home for the lonely and rejected
In love, safety and joy are a blanket

A better world
Only exists in love
That persists and pursues the broken to heal
Continuously whispers words of comfort

A better world
Is nothing but a selfless heart that gives up for others
Happy to receive last,
And selflessly serve for the benefit of others

A better world
Is nothing but unity of like minded people
Tirelessly fighting evil to create sustainable change
Laying down foundations of hope for the hopeless

A better world
Is in the hearts of leaders
From continent to continent, networking to share
And for growth.

give
her
a
voice

By Francis Mbewe
(Zambia)

GIVE HER A VOICE
by Francis Mbewe

Give her a voice,
And she will speak for all the brokenness
She sees, knows, feels and has feared to talk about

Give her a voice,
And she will speak through the struggles
She sees, has gone through and handles.

Give her a voice,
And hear visions of voices shut down
because of years of being called weak

Give her a voice,
And see how the strength that brings life
Can change them too

Give her a voice,
And change the story of future mothers
And their daughters.

purpose

By Emily Miki
(Cameroon)

PURPOSE
by Emily Miki

I am called to be free
I am free and fulfilled
I inspire and I lead

I am called to help free many
I am here to inspire
I am here to give hope

I am called to love
To love unconditionally
I am loved.

the
african
dream

By Dikeledi Mokoena
(South Africa)

THE AFRICAN DREAM
by Dikeledi Mokoena

The marrow in her bones is draped in eagerness
To nourish and fulfil African dreams deferred.
Their dreams,
Our dreams,
Nourish new paths for beings of the soil.
Minds ingrained with richness and potential,
Nothing limits great possibilities.

Each moment when the sun retires,
Collective hearts beat in unison,
The universe sprinkles seeds of greatness
Out of Africa's beautiful minds,
Pulsations in our palms birth visions of yesteryears.
We carve new dreams and never retire.
Each day at dawn,the earth dreams
Imbibing kola nuts in abundance for rebirth.

I see the sun dazzling upon a mighty Africa,
Beauty in its diversity,
Wealth in its presence.
Sound the kalanga to announce our dreams,
The ones who are not yet born are listening,
For the Adinkra to reverberate across these vast lands.
With each dream our feet vibrate,
Traversing rediscovery and the remembrance of setho sa rona.

imposter

By Rufaro Mudimu
(South Africa)

IMPOSTER
by Rufaro Mudimu

Out of the night,
Bright light.
Spotlight
Shining, revealing
For all to see
Me.

Should I be afraid,
Distressed
Or is this light
To be embraced?
Frozen in
Relentless light
Shining, revealing
For all to see
Me.

In the darkness
I built
With sureness and
Confidence.
But now
This light feels
Too bright
Shining, revealing
For too many to see
Me.

Who, what
How, why.
In the comfort
Of darkness
I could slowly,
Furtively
Build, break,
Try again,
Fumble for greatness,
And make mistakes,
Choosing slivers of light
To shine.
Sometimes.

I am overjoyed,
Afraid, terrified,
Uncomfortably
Buoyed
By this
Floodlight that
Shines, reveals
For me to see
Me.

"With being an Obama Leader and all that has come after, one of my greatest struggles has been with imposter syndrome, and the desire to hide from the spotlight. This poem is about that and dealing with the fear and discomfort that comes from receiving acknowledgement and praise, even after working hard and applying for it." ~ *Rufaro Mudimu*

the
blind
who
save

By Andrew Mukose
(Uganda)

THE BLIND WHO SAVE
by Andrew Mukose

Growing up with a single parent
My mother a University lecturer in Uganda
One day on her way back home
In a car accident she lost her sight
And her job as lecturer terminated

I wanted to end the suffering and stereotypes
that societies have towards the disabled
because its not only my mother
but more than 1.6 million people blind
In Uganda almost all disabled people unemployed
stigmatized and considered not productive

By luck I got a bursary to study
A bachelor's in medical and community-based rehabilitation
I realized blind people are geniuses
With a heightened sense of touch
They can detect breast cancer early
Once medically trained and equipped

In Uganda more than 50,000 women have breast cancer
More than 4,500 die annually

Gifted Hands Network impacts communities
Recruits and medically trains blind women
Certifies them as medical tactile examiners
Employs them in hospitals and clinics

We turn disability into a talent
An opportunity for blind people
Creating employment
Saving women from breast cancer
In hospitals and clinics
conducting early examinations
The blind who save.

Photo supplied by Gifted Hands Network

motherland

By *Thandiwe Mweetwa*
(Zambia)

MOTHERLAND
by Thandiwe Mweetwa

The endless sands of Sahara,
The snowy crown of Kilimanjaro,
The rolling plains of Serengeti,
The thunderous smoke of Mosi-oa-Tunya,
My Motherland gives me.

The soulful song of the fish eagle,
The wistful howl of the hyena,
The time-less roar of the lion,
The age-old wisdom of the elephant,
My Motherland gives me.

Fire-side wisdom,
The drumbeat that speaks to my soul,
A smile from a perfect stranger,
Seeming insurmountable odds,
My Motherland gives me.

Undying loyalty,
Unwavering commitment,
Unending belief in her greatness,
Unshakeable resolve to help her soar,
I give my Motherland.

a continent that carries hope

By Shikongeni Ntinda
(Namibia)

A CONTINENT THAT CARRIES HOPE
by Shikongeni Ntinda

It is possible - a prosperous Africa!

Moving across the continent
From South to North, East to West
The common denominator is natural resources endowment
From arable land to oil and diamonds
Nevermind our marine riches

Traveling the continent, what do we see?
Refugees camps are almost everywhere
People are foreigners in their mother continent
Civil wars have torn tribes apart
Abject poverty and the misery index are every day songs
Nevermind corruption and the glorification of criminals

Moving across the continent, what do we see?
Power struggle and transactional politics on boardrooms
agendas
Masses have lost hope and cry "who can rescue us?"
People seek refuge at dumpsites as a lender of last resort
They choose dumpsites instead of elected leaders
This is not a curse, it is what we have adopted

Dreaming across the continent, what do we see?
All hope is not lost
No one can better understand our challenges than us

We should believe in ourselves and say "**yes we can**"
Just as winter becomes summer

So we will turn our pain to power
So we will turn our problems into prosperity

A prosperous Africa. It is possible!

Photo supplied by Obama Foundation

a
better
world

By Mercy Odongo
(Kenya)

A BETTER WORLD
by Mercy Odongo

I envision a world

A world grounded on values

A people true to those values

Fairness and equity reigns

Dignity and value of humanity reigns

People inspired to be part of change

People play their part to realize the change

Leaders championing causes greater than themselves

Leaders who serve the public with diligence and guided by God.

all
of
us

By Paul Ojajuni
(Nigeria)

ALL OF US
by Paul Ojajuni

Sorrow, tears and blood; many stories untold
Hunger, famine and flood; hardest of times unfold
In the midst of plenty, poverty and inequality reigns
Just a few of us own what is meant for all of us

From one land to the next, we trade war like fabric
From one belief to the next, we peddle extremism like faith
One way or the other, we are guilty all the same
By standing, watching and not lending a voice for all of us

A collective voice of hope, truth, restoration and assurance,
That today we can secure now and tomorrow
To create a sustainable world of peace, tolerance and equity
For me, you and all of us

Like tributaries we all flow into the same sea,
A sea that will never run dry if we keep flowing in one direction
From the east, west, north and south
We are one and together stronger when we reflect all of us.

body
of
life

By Peter Okeugo
(Nigeria)

BODY OF LIFE
by Peter Okeugo

This body is my story
of pain and life
of hurt and love
of sadness and glory

This body is my canvas
of murals and painting
of art and sketch
and shattered pieces of glass

This body is my journey
of ups and downs
of back and forth
of rejection and acceptance

This body is my stamp
of bruises and scars
from African mosquitoes
and love bites

This body is my evidence
of fight for survival
of struggles and living
of dreams and hope

This body is me
of halftones and wholeness
of shame and courage
of weakness and strength

This body is me
of imperfection and hustles
This body is me
My body of life.

*This poem, Body of Life, tells a personal story
of the struggle for acceptance amidst the
anti-gay laws.*

Photo by Peter Okeugo

compassionate world

By Scheaffer Okore
(Kenya)

COMPASSIONATE WORLD
by Scheaffer Okore

One day, we will hold hands,
Seated on a rainbow rag,
Legs folded for a chat,
Eyes as windows,
Seeing.

One day, we will hold hands,
On the other side of acceptance,
Palms sweating annoyance,
Lungs full,
Breathing.

One day, we will hold hands,
Head resting on shoulder,
Stay still don't folder,
Fingers locked,
Believing.

One day, we will hold hands,
No explanation of existing,
Just declaration of being,
Persisting in silence,
Living.

One day, we will hold hands,
Infinitely with real chance,
Shielding us from soreness,
In a world of kindness,
Compassionate,
And selfless.

Photo supplied by the Obama Foundation

a
better
world

By Lea Razafimanitsony
(Madagascar)

A BETTER WORLD
by Lea Razafimanitsony

Even when days are hard and my dream seems to be far away from here
Even when struggles are trying to put me off
I won't give up, I'll be still and keep follow my dream
I'm dreaming of a better tomorrow,
Where adolescents and young people in the world are empowered
Where we all invest in their future,
Where we all join hands to rebuild a better world for our children
A better world where everything is possible,
where every single dream is possible
Where a beggar can see himself as a rich man,
where every child can choose what to do with their life

This is my letter to all youth in the world
Believe in yourself so you can make your dream come true
My why is to make you know your WHY?
Believe that you are amazing and unequalled
You can keep tomorrow always fresh in working on today as draft.

one
day

By Melene Rossouw
(South Africa)

ONE DAY
by Melene Rossouw

Out of the ashes a new nation was born
Building peace and democracy in scorn

Wounded we emerged from the plight
With only the hope of a better future in sight

A promise of freedom and dignity was offered
But hindsight... was the true meaning of this ever proffered?

Today we still live in abject poverty
Was this what you get by declaring national sovereignity?

A Constitution they uprightly adopted
To afford us all rights that they said were duly protected

Our people still persist to see the hope in the distant future perhaps
one day, one day... We will live a life free from all mental torture

As we stare through the cracked window of our lived reality
A pipe dream we got in exchange for our humanity

Can we continue this struggle they call a development trajectory?
Leading the masses down a path of misguided seductory

They said one day, one day we will have prosperity
But now we are starting to doubt their integrity

It is in this promise that we trust,
Though we ate nothing but the left over bread crust

Let freedom reign they say, but what is freedom if we can't escape
the painful reminders of poverty holding us captive every day

One day, one day they said...
As we lie and wait to be progressively led

Can I add my voice, can I have my say?
Well perhaps, one day, one day, they'll take us seriously
when we display our utter dismay

As a nation rose, the citizens will rise
And for once... Just once we will not compromise

One day...

Photo by Amanda Blankfield-Koseff

a
better
world

By Samuel J Sarr
(Togo)

A BETTER WORLD
by Samuel J Sarr

People far and wide let us come together,
No time to rest, no time to pass until things get better

Let us not throw our world away for another angel was born yesterday
If nothing is done today our heirs will have a hefty price to pay

Time to stand up now and face the facts
Only by working together can we achieve lasting impacts

Make this the day that together we vowed
To care for our environment and make our mothers proud

Let us be less about pollution
and more about solutions
Quality education now for every boy
and for every girl from here to Hanoi

Together we can effect the changes we want to see
Start where you are and believe that together we can achieve.

a
better
world

By Alero Thompson
(Nigeria)

A BETTER WORLD
by Alero Thompson

I see a world so full and few
I see a world so thick and thin
I see a world so cool and cold
I see a world so blue and black
I see a world so fair with fate
I see a world so loved with hate
I then see a better world so full, so thick,
  so cool, so blue, so fair and so loved.

hope
resides
in
love

By *Josef P van der Westhuizen*
(Namibia)

HOPE RESIDES IN LOVE
by Josef P van der Westhuizen

On a movie set, the expectation is for the director to shout CUT! CUT!
Absent are these words and present the scenes of injustice and inequality
that devours humanity
Clear that is in the eyes of the child, bare feet staring hopeless in the far
distance
Clear that is in the trembling voice of the elderly that speak hopelessness
In the walk of the young that is clear as the step further is unsure
And continuing is this;
Some are seizing all they can, most losing all they have and all they are

Hopeless the scenes seem and sad the outcome of these, these injustices
that has become epidemic
But amidst this epidemic glows a light that makes the hopelessness fade
away for drawn to the light we are
A glimmer that binds that which we regard as differences, that which we
regard as obstacles
The light shows bare that the difference is strength for it unites
It unites across race, tribe, gender or wealth, that glimmer that shines
through the heart and known through tongues as love

In that love we find Hope that humanity that rise beyond that which
causes injustice, that which causes unequal distribution of information,
of resources, of knowledge.
For in love we no longer first see your skin colour, your gender, we see
your humanity and the need to be there for each other

In that Hope for Africa for this world, some seizing what they can
no longer shall be for all will be equal to seize
In it most will not lose because only some seize it all
In it I, You, We will not lose who we are because someone else
chooses to oppress us to seize all
For in Love Hope for a better continent, for a better world,
for better humanity resides.

Photo supplied by the Obama Foundation

a
place
for
us
all

By Lesley Donna Williams
(South Africa)

A PLACE FOR US ALL
by Lesley Donna Williams

Just one stretch
An extended arm seeking rest
It grips an unsteady rock
Afraid to come tumbling down
Insecure about needing to descend
Success is the vision, foresight the mission
I frown as I propel myself up

Alas! I have arrived!
This ledge feels sturdy
Only to discover a confident dancer
Tap tap tapping away at the edge
I may lose balance
I scream out toward her
Not anticipating this state
She turns her face away from me
Whispering painfully
Who gave you permission to rise?

My self-doubt creeps in
I look deep within
Logically knowing that this is public space
How can I erase the anxiety raised
In questioning my own belonging?
There is a place for us all
If we share just a small piece of land

The rays of sunshine burgled my room, stealing the night away
I grabbed my smartphone before it let out a tone
Screaming across various time-zones
You see, while my work is local it hinges on global
I am transported into a virtual meeting presenting the best of the best

While technology excites crossing mental borders with delight
But physical borders and security mobsters
Tell me that my global village is a really big lie

Mirror mirror on the wall
Who is the most talented of us all?
Exclusion assists fake genius to persist
With several excluded from writing the test
Yet, manifesting the full potential of all is mutually beneficial
Creating a place for us all.

Photo supplied by Melene Rossouw

CONTRIBUTORS

Simidele Adeagbo
Nigeria

Olympian, Advocate, Entrepreneur

Passion: Building a better world through sport.

Moses Chubili
Zambia

Secretary General, Zambia Deaf Society

Passion: Inclusive development and inclusive leadership which benefits diverse groups of people in the communities.

Jean- Luc Agboyibo
Togo

Founder & President of Leading Youth, Sport and Development (LYSD)

Passion: Human Development - Helping children realise their potential.

Yaya Dama
Burkina Faso

Founder & CEO, Talk For Education

Passion: Every child deserves a quality education.

Edith Amin
Malawi

Humanitarian worker

Passion: Gender equality and social justice. She works to empower refugee girls, increase their access to quality education.

Paul Ekuru
Kenya

Media and Social Change Expert

Passion: Utilising design thinking to develop and execute innovative programs that raise youth community heroes across Kenya.

Amanda Blankfield-Koseff
South Africa

Founder & CEO, Empowervate Trust

Passion: To empower and motivate the next generation of active citizens.

Andrew Ihsaan Gasnolar
South Africa

Chairperson, Youth Economic Participation Programme

Passion: Issues of inequality, justice and the ongoing struggle to rebuild and ignite hope and possibility with boundless energy and commitment.

Dr Shakira Choonara
South Africa

African Union Youth Advisory Council

Passion: Healthcare, youth engagement and simply changing the world!

Temitope Isedowo
Nigeria

Co-founder, Lifting Youth and Fostering Entrepreneurship; Programmes Manager, AfriLabs

Passion: Technology, innovation and entrepreneurship in Africa.

CONTRIBUTORS continued

Joan Kabugu
Kenya

Founder, Ecila Films

Passion: "I believe authentic African stories have the ability to transform communities, countries and the continent."

Loyiso Kula
South Africa

Founder, Her.Issues

Passion: An advocate for gender balance, gender equality and gender parity in society. Loyiso is also inspired by the African continent and the dream of a borderless continent.

Thulile Khanyile
South Africa

Co-founder & Co-Executive Director, Nka'Thuto EduPropeller

Passion: Creating a society of problem solvers and technopreneurs through the use of STEMI principles.

Kudzai Kutukwa
South Africa

CEO & Co-founder, Mobbisurance

Passion: Using technology to make financial services affordable and accessible for everyone regardless of their income level.

Kenyi Yasin Abdallah Kenyi
South Sudan

Advocate and Legal Consultant Fidelity Law Chamber; Executive Director, TAHURID

Passion: Being true to myself and empowering or helping others find their passion.

Taryn Lock
South Africa

Co-Founder & Executive Director, Read to Rise

Passion: To create positive social change through literacy, social development and art.

Jonathan Kingwill
South Africa

Entrepreneur, ClockWork App

Passion: Solving African problems, particularly through technology.

Innocent Magambi
Burundi

Founder & Executive Director, There is Hope

Passion: "My passion is to see refugees included in development agenda of their host country."

Lucky Komba
Tanzania

Executive Producer, Well Told Story

Passion: Telling stories to inspire and revive hopes.

Mabatho Makatla
Lesotho

Manager of Operations, Sepheo

Passion: To ensure that children live in loving homes and reintegrating street children back into families, by offering psychosocial support to ensure that children are retained in the community.

CONTRIBUTORS continued

Francis Mbewe
Zambia

Founder & CEO, Kukula Fund

Passion: Investing in women and girls to build a better world.

Thandiwe Mweetwe
Zambia

Senior Ecologist/Education Manager, Zambian Carnivore Programme

Passion: Helping Africa's people and wildlife to thrive side by side.

Emily Miki
Cameroon

Co-Founder & Executive Director, Denis Miki Foundation and Efeti Ventures

Passion: Building the capacities of less privileged persons especially those living in rural and conflict affected communities through economic and livelihood support.

Shikongeni Ntinda
Namibia

Chief Economist at the Ministry of Industrialisation, Trade and SME Development

Passion: Business and community development.

Dikeledi Mokoena
South Africa

Founder, AfroUsawa: Woman for Public Leadership; Global Youth Chairperson of the Pan-African Federalist movement.

Passion: Uniting Africa and facilitating women's entry into political leadership.

Mercy Odongo
Kenya

Foreign Service Officer / Diplomat at Ministry of Foreign Affairs Kenya

Passion: Strategic visioning, exercising adaptive leadership, building partnerships, and getting things done in a development context.

Rufaro Mudimu
South Africa

CEO, enke

Passion: To create environments where people can identify, define and achieve success on their own terms.

Paul Ojajuni
Nigeria

Co-Founder & Director, Research and Development HACEY Health Initiative

Passion: Addressing unmet health needs of underserved population.

Andrew Mukose
Uganda

Founder & CEO, Gifted Hands Network

Passion: To recruit and medically train visually impaired women to become certified medical tactile examiners that conduct early breast cancer detection.

Peter Okeugo
Nigeria

US-based Nigerian freelance journalist and LGBT rights activist.

Passion: His reporting on LGBT issues in Africa exposed the human rights abuses that LGBT people face on the continent.

CONTRIBUTORS continued

Scheaffer Okore
Kenya

Vice Chairperson, Ukweli Party

Passion: Humanizing women and all other minority persons.

Josef P van der Westhuizen
Namibia

Representative Council Chairperson
National Youth Council of Namibia

Passion: "It gives me great fulfillment and pleasure to help another and see growth of any amount in their lives."

Lea Razafimanitsony
Madagascar

Strategic and Independent Consultant

Passion: Youth empowerment. "I think that when we invest in young people we can believe in a better future."

Lesley Donna Williams
South Africa

CEO, Tshimologong Digital Innovation Precinct

Passion: Believes that living your full potential is a basic human right and strives to create this opportunity through all her work.

Melene Rossouw
South Africa

Executive Director, Women Lead Movement

Passion: Educating, empowering and advocating for social and political change by utilising the constitution as a tool to effect such transformation.

Samuel J Sarr
Togo

Founder & Executive Director, Kailend

Passion: Environmental conservation, renewable energy and learning about new subjects.

Alero Thompson
Nigeria

Chief Education officer/Founder of Blue Sands Academy

Passion: Girl child development and a clean environment for all to live in.